NBA HOT SHOTS

by JOE LAYDEN

SCHOLASTIC INC.

NEW YORK   TORONTO   LONDON   AUCKLAND   SYDNEY

Photo Credits
Cover (Abdur-Rahim): NBA/Christopher J. Relke. **Cover (Cassell), 8, 12, 20:** NBA/Nathaniel S. Butler. **Cover (Finley), 10:** NBA/Glenn James. **3, 6:** NBA/Andrew D. Bernstein. **4, 22:** NBA/Andy Hayt. **14:** NBA/Norm Perdue. **16:** NBA/Tim O'Dell. **18:** NBA/Fernando Medina.

ISBN 0-590-06056-2

© 1999 by NBA Properties, Inc.
All rights reserved. Published by Scholastic Inc.

12 11 10 9 8 7 6 5 4 3 2 1   9/9 0 1 2 3 4/0

Printed in the U.S.A.
First Scholastic printing, February 1999
Book design: Michael Malone

ON FIRE!

Every team needs at least one special player. Someone who can light up the scoreboard and bring fans to their feet! Maybe he's a dazzling little point guard with magical moves. Maybe he's a great outside shooter. Whatever his specialty, this much is certain:

When he's HOT, no one can stop him.

The players in this book represent ten different teams and several positions. But they share at least one common trait: attitude. When offense is really needed, these guys want the ball in their hands. With a no-look pass, a three-point bomb, or a rim-rattling dunk, they can change the course of a game.

They are the NBA's hot shots.

3

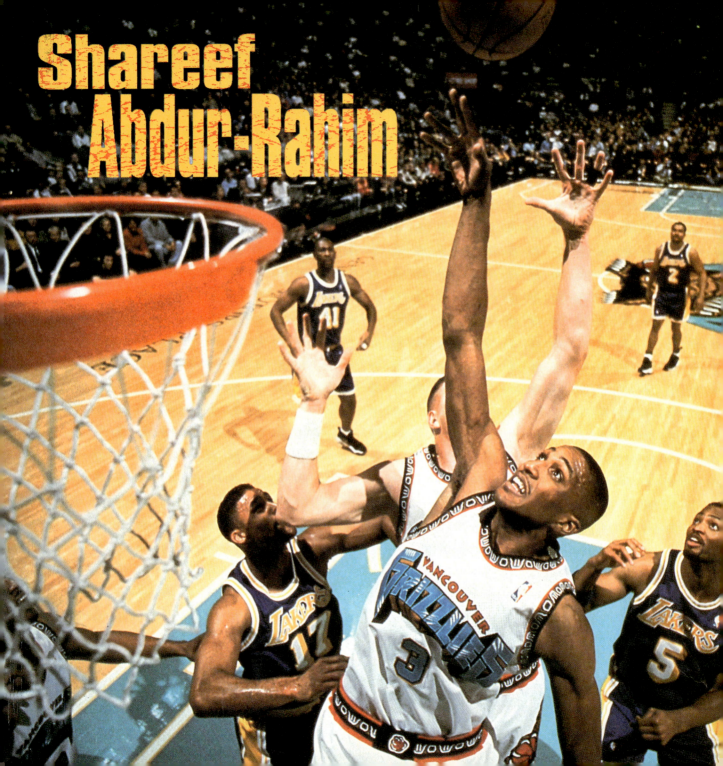

Shareef
Abdur-Rahim

His Game Does the Talking

When the Vancouver Grizzlies selected Shareef Abdur-Rahim with the third pick in the 1996 NBA Draft, some observers questioned the choice. After all, he was only 19 years old and had played just one season of college basketball. But it wasn't long before "Reef" proved that he was ready for the big time. The versatile forward led his team in scoring and was named to the Schick NBA All-Rookie first team. Since then he has become one of the NBA's best all-around players. Thirty-point outbursts are common for Shareef. But those are the only kind of outbursts you'll see from him. Shareef is one of the most polite and modest players in the league.

DID YOU KNOW? SHAREEF HOLDS SINGLE-SEASON GRIZZLIES RECORDS FOR SCORING (1,806) AND MINUTES (2,907).

Kobe Bryant

Kobe Bryant	POSITION	HEIGHT	WEIGHT	BIRTH DATE
	Guard	6-6	200	8/23/78

Rising Star

Not since Michael Jordan first came to the NBA has a young player generated such excitement. In fact, with his spectacular athletic ability and his desire to succeed, Kobe Bryant reminds a lot of people of Air Jordan. But Kobe does things his own way. Shortly after leading Lower Merion High School to a Pennsylvania state championship in 1996, Kobe decided to turn professional. That fall, just two months and eleven days after his 18th birthday, he became the youngest player ever to appear in an NBA game. Since then Kobe has won the Nestlé Crunch Slam Dunk contest and been voted a starter in the NBA All-Star Game.

KOBE'S FATHER, JOE "JELLY BEAN" BRYANT, WAS ALSO A BASKETBALL PLAYER. HE SPENT EIGHT YEARS IN THE NBA BEFORE MOVING TO EUROPE TO PLAY PROFESSIONALLY.

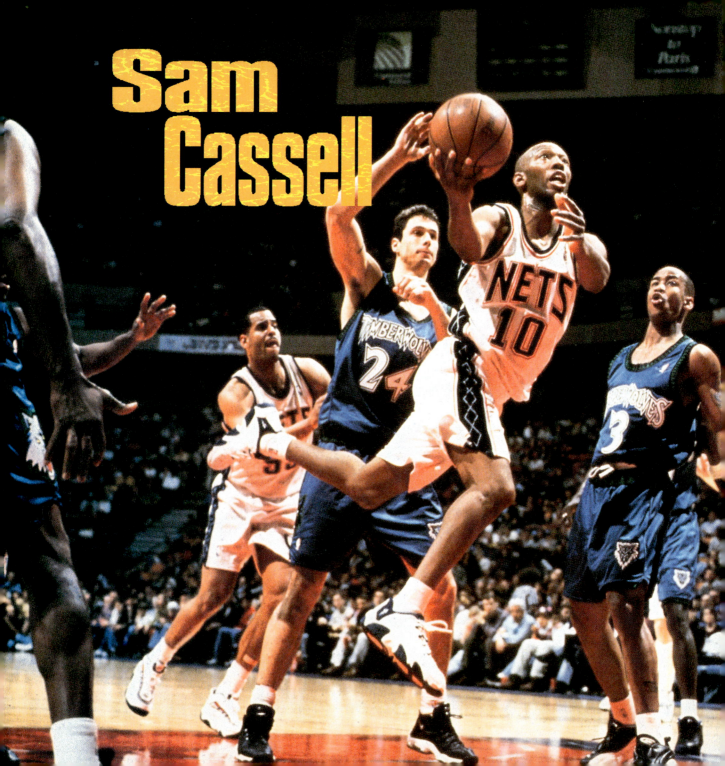

Sam
Cassell

Sam Cassell	POSITION	HEIGHT	WEIGHT	BIRTH DATE
	Guard	6-3	185	11/18/69

Instant Offense

Sam Cassell's job is to run the offense, and he does it about as well as anyone in the NBA. Like most great point guards, he takes as much pride in delivering a perfect pass as he does in hitting a jump shot. But when the New Jersey Nets really need a basket, they often turn to Sam. Slippery and smart, he's capable of sparking an offense in a hurry. In the second half of a February, 1998, game against the Vancouver Grizzlies, for example, Sam scored 26 points! When he's hot, he's almost unstoppable. An intense competitor, Sam helped lead the Houston Rockets to consecutive NBA championships in 1994 and 1995.

DID YOU KNOW? SAM ATTENDED DUNBAR HIGH SCHOOL IN BALTIMORE, MARYLAND, WHICH ALSO PRODUCED SEVERAL OTHER NBA PLAYERS, INCLUDING POINT GUARD MUGGSY BOGUES.

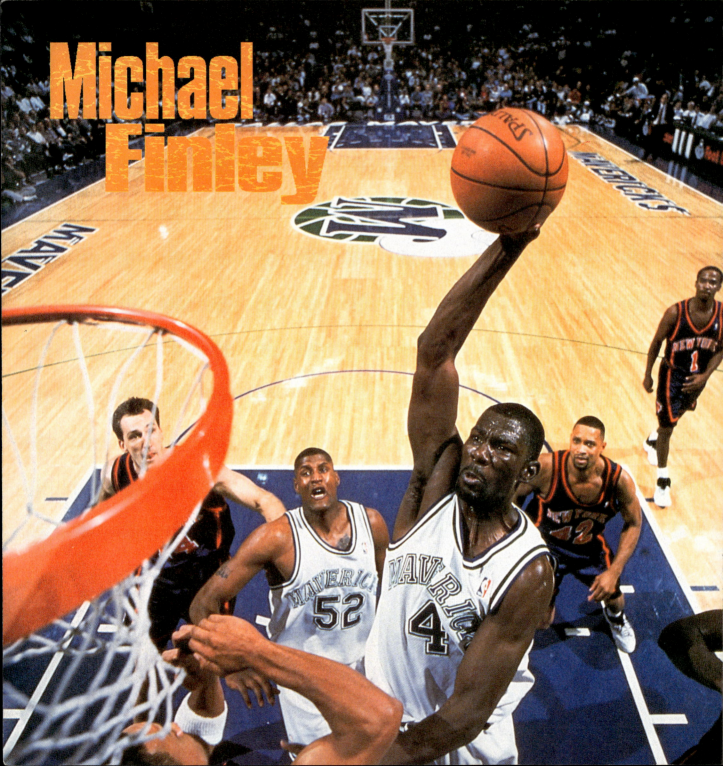

Michael Finley

Michael Finley	POSITION	HEIGHT	WEIGHT	BIRTH DATE
	Guard	6-7	215	3/6/73

The Iron Man

Michael Finley was almost overlooked in the 1995 NBA Draft. In fact, 20 players were taken ahead of him. But Michael never doubted his ability, and it wasn't long before everyone knew he had a real game. He soared to a second place finish in the 1996 Nestlé Crunch Slam Dunk competition and was named to the Schick NBA All-Rookie first team. Few players have Michael's combination of size and quickness. He's at his best in the open floor, directing a fast break. But he can also nail the outside jumper or take his defender to the hole. Michael is one of the toughest players in the league. In three seasons, he's never missed a game.

DID YOU KNOW? AS A HIGH SCHOOL SENIOR, MICHAEL WON A CONTEST IN WHICH THE GRAND PRIZE WAS AN OPPORTUNITY TO PLAY A GAME OF ONE-ON-ONE AGAINST MICHAEL JORDAN.

Allen Iverson	POSITION	HEIGHT	WEIGHT	BIRTH DATE
	Guard	6-0	165	6/7/75

CatchMe
If You Can

Size has never been an issue for Allen Iverson. Just ask anyone who has ever tried to guard him. Although barely six feet tall and slender as a toothpick, the Philadelphia 76ers point guard is one of the NBA's most spectacular offensive players. He can electrify a crowd with a three-point shot or a windmill jam. But his favorite move is a lightning-quick crossover dribble that often leaves opponents tripping over their own feet. It's no wonder that when Allen has the ball, excitement fills the air. He was named the 1996–97 Schick NBA Rookie of the Year and has been one of the league's top scorers in each of his two seasons.

DID YOU KNOW? ALLEN BECAME THE FIRST SIXER SINCE CHARLES BARKLEY TO FINISH IN THE TOP 10 IN SCORING IN CONSECUTIVE SEASONS.

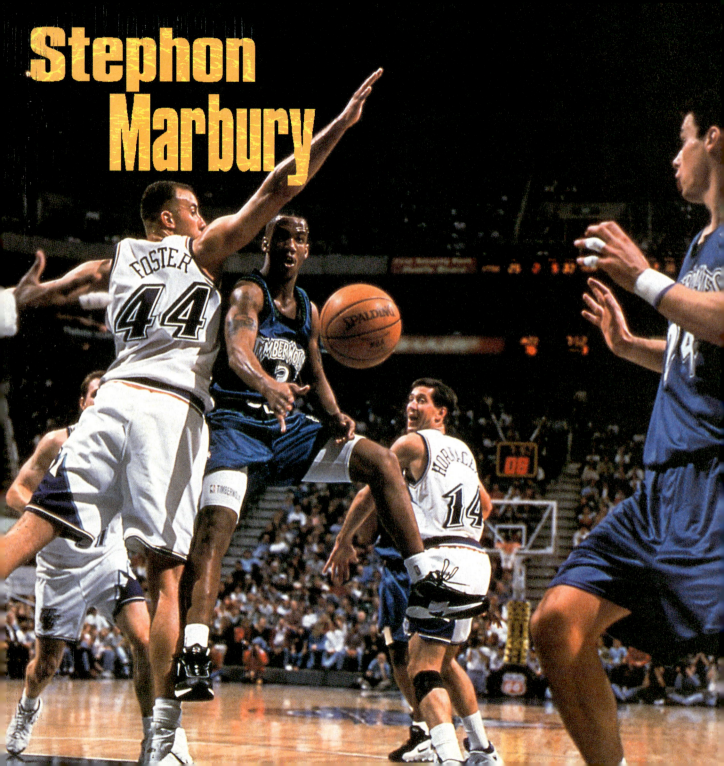

Stephon
Marbury

Stephon Marbury	POSITION	HEIGHT	WEIGHT	BIRTH DATE
	Guard	6-2	180	2/20/77

The Play maker

When you grow up in a basketball family, expectations are high. That's the way it was for Stephon Marbury. After all, three of his brothers and two of his sisters played college ball. But Stephon turned out to be the best of the bunch. He was named national player of the year as a senior in high school. Then, after just one year at Georgia Tech, he jumped to the NBA. With Stephon running the show at point guard, the Minnesota Timberwolves have become one of the NBA's hottest young teams. He helped lead the team to their first-ever playoff appearance. Whether he's leading a fast break or calmly directing a half-court offense, Stephon plays with the confidence of a veteran.

DID YOU KNOW? AS A ROOKIE, STEPHON ONCE HAD 17 ASSISTS IN A SINGLE GAME.

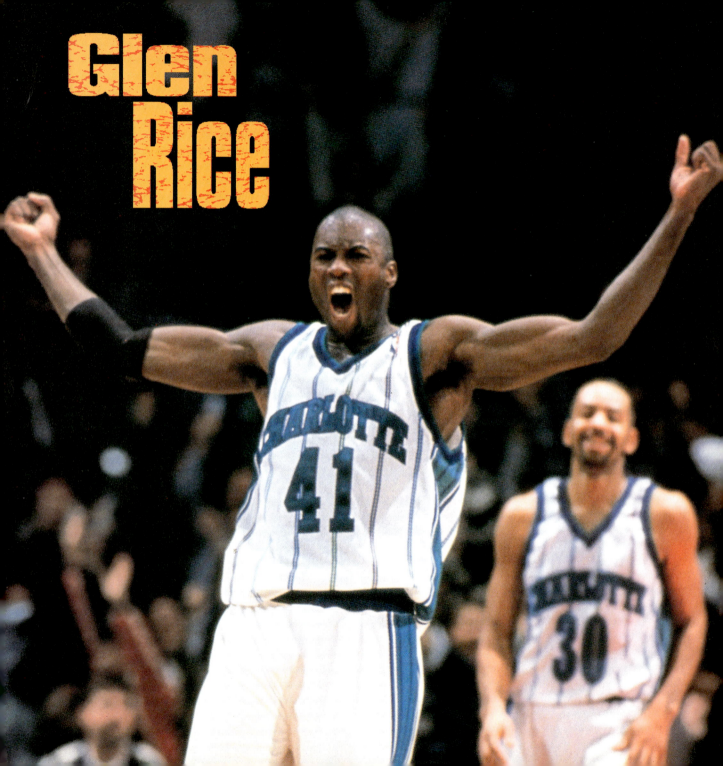

Glen
Rice

Glen Rice	POSITION	HEIGHT	WEIGHT	BIRTH DATE
Forward	6-8	220	5/8/67

The Sure Shot

How do you stop Glen Rice? If you guard him too closely, he'll glide past you and take the ball right to the basket. If you give him any breathing room, he'll step back and hit a three-point shot. No wonder they call him "G Money." When he has the ball, it's like money in the bank. Glen has been tearing up NBA defenses for nine years. Some nights it seems as though he simply can't miss. Like the time he scored 56 points against the Orlando Magic! During the 1997 All-Star Game he erupted for 20 points in the third quarter and was named Most Valuable Player.

DID YOU KNOW? GLEN'S CAREER SCORING AVERAGE IS NEARLY 21 POINTS PER GAME, AND HIS SHOOTING PERCENTAGE FROM THREE-POINT RANGE IS ALWAYS AMONG THE BEST IN THE LEAGUE.

Glenn Robinson	POSITION	HEIGHT	WEIGHT	BIRTH DATE
	Forward	6-7	235	1/10/73

The BigDog

Glenn Robinson is the type of player every team would love to have. In 1994 he won the John Wooden Award as the nation's top college basketball player. Then he was the first player taken in the 1994 NBA Draft. It proved to be a smart pick by the Milwaukee Bucks. In 1994–95 Glenn led all first-year players in scoring and was named to the Schick NBA All-Rookie first team. An injury prevented Glenn from competing in the 1996 Olympic Games, but with a scoring average of 21.5 per game, he continues to be one of the NBA's most feared offensive players. This is one big dog whose bite is worse than his bark!

DID YOU KNOW? GLENN RANKED SECOND IN THE NBA IN MINUTES PER GAME (41.0).

John
Starks

John Starks	POSITION	HEIGHT	WEIGHT	BIRTH DATE
	Guard	6-5	185	8/10/65

The Energizer

When the New York Knicks need instant offense, they turn to John Starks. The energetic guard with the fiery personality knows how to ignite a rally. Perhaps that's because he's never been a quitter. John wasn't even drafted when his college career ended, and he spent parts of two seasons trying to make it to the NBA. The Knicks gave him an opportunity in 1990, and John made the most of it. A gifted long-range shooter who also has great leaping ability, John has a reputation for giving his teammates an emotional boost when they need it most. He's often the spark that lights the fire.

DID YOU KNOW? JOHN WON THE NBA SIXTH MAN AWARD IN 1997.

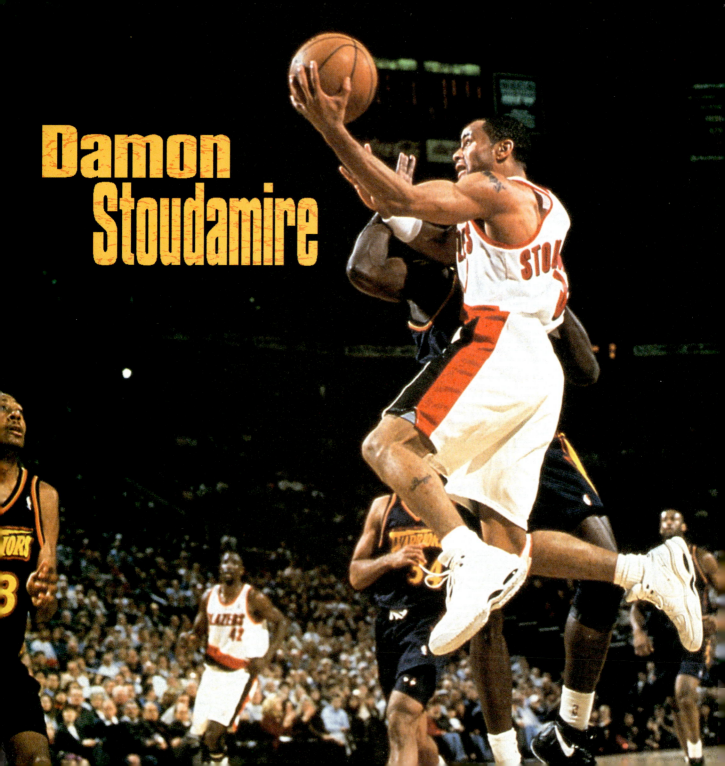

Damon
Stoudamire

Damon Stoudamire	POSITION	HEIGHT	WEIGHT	BIRTH DATE
	Guard	5-10	171	9/3/73

Good Things come in Small Packages

On Damon Stoudamire's right arm is a tattoo of Mighty Mouse holding a basketball. It's his way of reminding everyone that little guys can be heroes, too. A slick ballhandler with great quickness, Damon has become one of the NBA's best point guards. He proved that he could survive in the land of the giants by playing more than 40 minutes a game in his first season. Now with the Portland Trail Blazers, Damon is an exciting player who can bust up a defense with a pass or a shot. At 5-10, he's one of the smallest players in the league. But no one has a bigger heart.

DID YOU KNOW? DAMON WAS NAMED 1995—96 SCHICK NBA ROOKIE OF THE YEAR.

Quickie Quiz

1. He's the youngest player to ever appear in an NBA game.

2. He once scored 56 points in a single game.

3. He went to the same high school as Muggsy Bogues.

4. His favorite move is the crossover dribble.

5. He's known as one of the NBA's best coming off the bench.

6. At 5-10, he's one of the smallest players in the NBA.

7. He didn't miss a game in his first three seasons.

8. He was selected before Jason Kidd and Grant Hill in the 1994 NBA Draft.

9. His nickname is "Reef."

10. He helped lead Minnesota to their first-ever playoff berth.

A. Shareef Abdur-Rahim

B. Kobe Bryant

C. Sam Cassell

D. Michael Finley

E. Allen Iverson

F. Stephon Marbury

G. Glen Rice

H. Glenn Robinson

I. John Starks

J. Damon Stoudamire

ANSWERS: 1-B, 2-G, 3-C, 4-E, 5-I, 6-J, 7-D, 8-H, 9-A, 10-F.